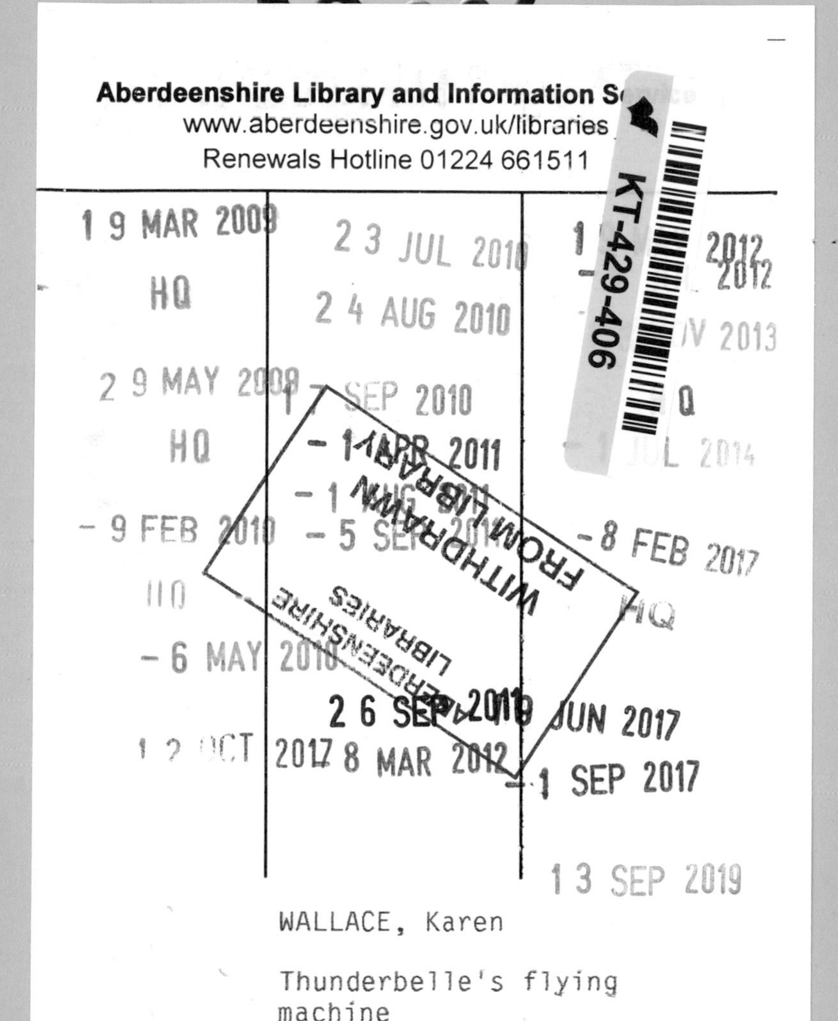

Aberdeenshire Library and Information Service
www.aberdeenshire.gov.uk/libraries
Renewals Hotline 01224 661511

KT-429-406

WITHDRAWN FROM LIBRARY
ABERDEENSHIRE LIBRARIES

WALLACE, Karen

Thunderbelle's flying machine

ALIS
2619367

For Oscar Birkbeck
K.W.
For Sonny and Nia,
With love
G. P-R.

First published in 2007 by Orchard Books
First paperback publication in 2008

ORCHARD BOOKS
338 Euston Road, London NW1 3BH
Orchard Books Australia
Level 17/207 Kent St, Sydney, NSW 2000

ISBN 978 1 84362 622 0 (hardback)
ISBN 978 1 84362 630 5 (paperback)

Text © Karen Wallace 2007
Illustrations © Guy Parker-Rees 2007

The rights of Karen Wallace and Guy Parker-Rees to be identified as the author and illustrator of this work have been asserted by them in accordance with the Copyright, Designs and Patents Act, 1988.

1 3 5 7 9 10 8 6 4 2 (hardback)
1 3 5 7 9 10 8 6 4 2 (paperback)

Printed in China

Orchard Books is a division of Hachette Children's Books, an Hachette Livre UK company.

www.orchardbooks.co.uk

Monster Mountain

Thunderbelle's Flying Machine

Karen Wallace

Illustrated by

Guy Parker-Rees

ABERDEENSHIRE LIBRARY AND INFORMATION SERVICES	
2619367	
HJ	667509
JS	£4.99
JU	JF

"I want to fly," said Thunderbelle. "I want to look down and see my house from the sky."

"But you're a monster," said Clodbuster. "Monsters don't fly."

"Pipsquawk can fly," said Thunderbelle.
"But she's half bat," said Clodbuster.

Thunderbelle didn't answer. She made herself some wings.

She pulled the straps and the wings went up and down. She pulled harder and harder and the wings flapped faster and faster. But nothing happened.

"What have I done wrong?" cried Thunderbelle.

Clodbuster scratched his head.

"Maybe they have to be bat wings."

Thunderbelle rang the Brilliant Ideas gong. **Bong! Bong! Bong!**

The other monsters came as fast as they could. Roxorus skidded by on his skateboard.

Mudmighty slid down on a cabbage leaf.

Pipsquawk landed on a low branch.

"What's the brilliant idea?" cried Roxorus.

"I want to fly!" cried Thunderbelle.

"What about a giant catapult?"
said Mudmighty.

"What happens when I land?" asked Thunderbelle.
"A great big BUMP!" said Mudmighty.

"That's not a brilliant idea," said Thunderbelle.

“What about a cannon?” cried Clodbuster.

“What happens when you light it?” asked Thunderbelle.
“An enormous BANG!” cried Clodbuster.

“That’s not a brilliant idea,” said Thunderbelle.

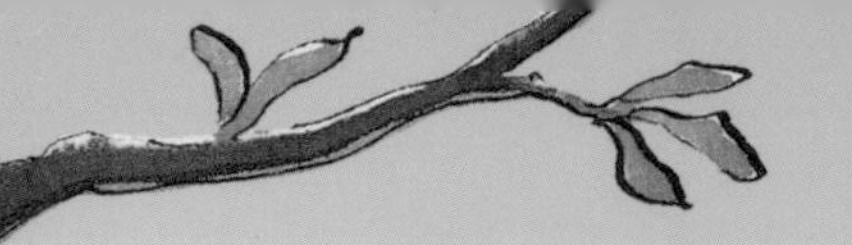

Pipsquawk flapped down from
her branch.
"We'll build you an aeroplane!"

Thunderbelle jumped up and down and the ground shook.
"Pipsquawk, you're a genius!"

A Thunderbelle-sized aeroplane would need to be very big.
All the monsters offered to help.

Roxorus found round
stones for the wheels.

Clodbuster brought wood
and a pot of paint
from his house.

Mudmighty picked beetroot leaves for the wings. Thunderbelle liked the pink bits in them.

Pipsquawk collected sticks and feathers and pieces of shell. All morning the monsters hammered and glued and painted.

Thunderbelle went to make them some lunch.
When she came back, she nearly dropped her tray of strawberry jam sandwiches.

There was a really cool aeroplane in her garden!

After lunch, Thunderbelle put on a flying suit, a helmet and a pair of goggles. She sat in the pilot's seat.

"It's easy," said Clodbuster.
"All you do is push the shell, flip the stick and twirl the feather. Then, VROOM! You're off!"

Thunderbelle didn't move.
"What's wrong?" shouted
the others.

"I forgot I'm afraid of heights!"
Thunderbelle wailed.

The other monsters didn't know what to say.
Everyone had worked so hard on the aeroplane.

"Don't cry, Thunderbelle," said
Pipsquawk.
"Anyone can be afraid of heights."
"What am I going to do-o-o-o?"
wailed Thunderbelle.

Pipsquawk swung back and forth
and thought hard.
"I know what to do!" she squawked.
"We'll turn the aeroplane into
a swing!"

First Pipsquawk found
the perfect tree.

Then Mudmighty pulled
up some vines.

Clodbuster and Roxorus made two thick ropes.

At last they hung the aeroplane from the tree. The swing was ready!

Thunderbelle climbed into the pilot's seat.
The other monsters gave her a great big PUSH!

Thunderbelle soared into the air and whooped with joy.

"My aeroplane is the best swing ever!"

THUNDERBELLE'S NEW HOME	ISBN 978 1 84362 626 8
THUNDERBELLE'S SPOOKY NIGHT	ISBN 978 1 84362 625 1
THUNDERBELLE'S BAD MOOD	ISBN 978 1 84362 629 9
THUNDERBELLE'S PARTY	ISBN 978 1 84362 627 5
THUNDERBELLE'S FLYING MACHINE	ISBN 978 1 84362 630 5
THUNDERBELLE'S SONG	ISBN 978 1 84362 628 2
THUNDERBELLE'S BEAUTY PARLOUR	ISBN 978 1 84362 631 2
THUNDERBELLE GOES TO THE MOVIES	ISBN 978 1 84362 632 9

All priced at £4.99. Monster Mountain books are available from all good bookshops, or can be ordered direct from the publisher: Orchard Books, PO BOX 29, Douglas IM99 1BQ. Credit card orders please telephone 01624 836000 or fax 01624 837033 or visit our website: www.orchardbooks.co.uk or e-mail: bookshop@enterprise.net for details.

To order please quote title, author and ISBN and your full name and address. Cheques and postal orders should be made payable to 'Bookpost plc.' Postage and packing is FREE within the UK (overseas customers should add £2.00 per book).

Prices and availability are subject to change.